His Healing Love

His Healing Love

A visual journey of healing in truth

Written, Illustrated, and Published by

Mae Danielle

His Healing Love. A visual journey of healing

This Book is Dedicated to

Daddy Almighty, my Lord and Savior

Author's Preface

Art has always been a way for me to express my feelings when the words are hard to say. And over the years the Lord has used my art by giving me images that express His love and truth to me. Just the process of drawing out an image helps me to believe and accept what He is speaking to me.

In sharing my art with a few friends, they encouraged me to create a book of my work. Following their advice, my intention was that the book would be just the artwork with corresponding scriptures. However, during the process of creating the book, the people I shared with wanted to know more; they wanted the backstory behind each picture. I was hesitant to include details of my journey because I didn't want the trauma I had suffered to steal the spotlight from the message of Christ's glorious healing love. I also didn't want the readers to feel as though they had to relate to specific struggles I have had in order to apply the images and Scriptures to their own healing.

I trust that in spite of my concerns, it is the Lord's will for me to share my journey. It is my prayer that every reader will be touched in some way by Christ's love and healing grace. All the glory belongs to Him!

Acknowledgement Page

I owe an incredible debt of gratitude to a number of people who have spoken into my life, prayed for me, provided advice, helped, or walked beside me on my journey.

First, I am forever grateful for my spiritual mother, Mary Lyn Bartek. I thank you the most for teaching me how to hear, feel, and see the love of our Heavenly Father. Thank you for walking beside me, and calling me a "walking little miracle." Thank you for loving me unconditionally even in my brokenness. Last but certainly not least, thank you for encouraging me to grow and share His unfailing love with others.

I want to thank Janet Johnston for graciously editing and working so patiently with me in the long process of creating this book.

A special thank you to my own beautiful little miracle, my daughter Kaytlyn Floyd. You encourage me every day to just live life fully and blindly keep walking in faith. You have a special gift of taking impairment and turning it around into empowerment. I am truly blessed to be your mom.

Additionally, a special thank you to my Michael Kunze for your unconditional love, your prayers, and support throughout the publishing process.

Thank you, Pastor Dave Besecker, for encouraging me to step out in faith to share my art with others.

Thank you to my Bestie, Diane Ocker, for always encouraging me and walking alongside me.

Thank you, Annie Yorty, for your wisdom, expertise, and support.

My sincere gratitude to my church family at Otterbein Church, my small group family, and my forever family with Celebrate Recovery for your countless prayers, loves, and support.

Lastly, I would like to thank Dr Thomas Gardner for your professional advice and support on bringing this book to completion.

Prologue

The small child ran as fast as she could to hide in the woods. She didn't stop until she found the tallest tree. Looking up at it she wiped the tears from her face and combed her fingers through her tangled hair. She brushed the mud and grass off her clothes, hoping she looked good enough. As she carefully ascended the tall tree she could feel her hope ascending as well. *He <u>has</u> to hear me this time, she thought. I will be so close to heaven He has to hear me.* As she reached the top, clinging to her renewed hope, she closed her eyes and spoke loudly to the heavens, "Please God, I want to be loved. I want to be a good girl. I don't want to be in trouble all the time anymore. Nobody likes me, nobody will be my friend. I'm not smart; I keep messing up and they say I should know better. Please God, I don't want to be stupid anymore. I want to be pretty too, God. I don't like it when they make fun of me and call me names. God, can you answer my prayers if you're not too busy, please? Please make me a little girl they will want and love, and that I will have lots of friends. Pretty please, God. In Jesus' name I pray, amen."

The little girl waited quietly at the top of the tree until the sky began to darken. She didn't hear God's voice. All she heard was the wind rustling the leaves. As rain began to fall, so too did her hope, accompanied by the silent tears that had formed in her heart. 'I suppose God doesn't like me either,' she thought. 'They did say He doesn't like bad little girls.' The rain fell faster as she climbed down the tree. Amidst blowing leaves swirling around her, and loud claps of thunder, she raced home, her thoughts and emotions reflecting the turmoil and darkness of the storm.

I believe the heavens wept that night. God didn't create this little one to be anyone else; He loved her just the way she was. A battle for this little girl's heart was being fought across the realms as the Lord Almighty, her Daddy Almighty, fought valiantly for her.

The Lord is near all who cry out to him, all who cry out to him sincerely. Psalm 145:18 (NET)

Table of contents

Chapter 1

The Damaging Roots

In this world you will have trouble.

John 16:33b (NIV)

Although I cried out to God from many treetops, I was not rescued or miraculously changed into someone else during my childhood. But the rescue and the miracle came. For though my story began in a dark world of chaos and trauma, my real story has become about what God has done for me.

Yes, the sins of my abusers and the evils they committed impacted me, but they no longer define me. Only God has the power and the authority to define me accurately, and He has revealed His truths and shown me my true identity!

> *If you exploit them in any way*
>
> *and they cry out to me,*
>
> *then I will certainly hear their cry.*
>
> *Exodus 22:23 (NLT)*

The trauma I survived, however, affected my childhood development. The scars from emotional, physical, and childhood abuse left me with feelings of abandonment and rejection. But God's healing love is so much greater than all of this. At age eighteen I was diagnosed as mentally disabled and placed in adult foster care. That label led to many hospitals and treatment centers where my pent-up anger was released. I refused to accept the label I'd been given and so refused help from anyone. I lost any desire to live until one day, locked in a room for my safety, I felt God's Spirit holding me and whispering that He would help me. That marked the starting point of my healing, and now serves as a reminder of how very far my Daddy Almighty has brought me as an overcomer. He defines me as "saved" and calls me His "beloved child."

You meant to hurt me.

But God turned your evil into good.

It was to save the lives of many people.

And it is being done.

Genesis 50:20 (ICB)

Childhood sexual abuse convinced me that it was wrong and unsafe to desire any kind of touch from another person. So Daddy Almighty looked with me again and again at many memories of my abuse so that I might become convinced that the sexual abuse wasn't my fault. In this powerful and loving way, He showed me that my innocent desires for comfort and affection did not cause the abuse. He showed me that it was caused by the evil desires of adult predators who chose to defile and assault me, instead of protecting me.

I wasn't created wrongly! My Creator made me with desires for love, comfort and affection. I've learned that when a child's basic emotional needs aren't met, the child will search to fulfill those needs and accept whatever morsel of affection they encounter; yes, even if it also brings harm to them.

I was once broken, but now His love is the thread holding my shattered self together. May His light shine brightly through my repaired seams.

The Lord answered,
"Could a mother forget a child
who nurses at her breast?
Could she fail to love an infant who
came from her own body?
Even if a mother could forget,
I will never forget you."
Isaiah 49:15 (CEV)

Why me? A simple question carrying a heavy load of pain and heartache. I look back at my childhood looking for any clues, a reason, an answer to why. Why did they not like me? Why did so many choose to abuse me? What was it about me that made them want to harm me? Was I really that bad? Was I ugly? Was I dirty or smelly? What was wrong with me? Why wouldn't I assume that it was my fault when harm found me so often? Daddy Almighty declares that it wasn't my fault. Even the world says it's not a child's fault. As He leads me away from the fruitless path of why, He whispers

"They failed to love you unconditionally."

Love never gives up.

Love cares more for others than for self.

Love doesn't want what it doesn't have.

Love doesn't strut,

Doesn't have a swelled head,

Doesn't force itself on others,

Isn't always "me first,"

Doesn't fly off the handle,

Doesn't keep score of the sins of others,

Doesn't revel when others grovel,

Takes pleasure in the flowering of truth,

Puts up with anything, Trusts God always,

Always looks for the best,

Never looks back,

But keeps going to the end.

1 Corinthians 13:4-8 (MSG)

Everything's falling apart on me, God; put me together again with your Word.

Psalm 119:107 (MSG)

Like a fragile egg teetering on a narrow ledge, I tried holding it all inside. Though internally I felt overwhelmed by my fear of cracking and completely falling apart, I desperately wanted to be seen as "normal".

To me, normal meant I could handle everything that came into my life. So pushed and shoved aside, I'd hide my tears again and again, hardening myself more with each passing storm. I stuffed feeling after feeling deep inside, silently wondering who am I that I should even matter at all. My life was nothing more than a shell of an existence, at the very most.

But one held-back tear too many, and the dam burst, pushing me over the edge. I came crashing down, shattering into pieces as I hit solid ground. There were no king's horses or king's men . . . but instead, there was the King Himself. The King of Kings picked me up and started putting me back together again.

Deep in your heart
you cried out to the Lord.
Now let your tears overflow
your walls day and night.
Don't ever lose hope
or let your tears stop.
Get up and pray for help
all through the night.
Pour out your feelings to the Lord.

Lamentations 2:18-19a (CEV)

. . . You are precious and
honored in my sight . . .
because I love you.
Isaiah 43:4 (NIV)

The first step in His healing love was for me to see Him as my Daddy Almighty, and myself as His little one. This was a gigantic step of faith for me to take. In my adult world I have lived as a strong, independent single mom with a wonderful special needs child. And even though I have no family members close by, I have been reluctant to ask anyone for help or admit that I needed it. These are the reasons I told myself that I couldn't step into a child like faith.

However, the reasons that were hidden deeply within me are exactly why Daddy Almighty insisted that I take this step of faith. Deep inside I still had the same feelings as that little girl hiding in the woods, running amuck in her own self-conceived little world because her real world was sad, lonely, scary, demanding, and stressful. Inwardly, I was still struggling with feeling abandoned, rejected, and unloved.

Daddy Almighty knew my healing journey needed to begin at the root of that wounded little-girl heart. He wanted me to go beyond the facade of my adult self to experience Him as that small and vulnerable little child who is loved, wanted, and taken care of. He wanted me to grow to trust in His love so that I could keep choosing to believe He is always with me and for me, even when it felt like just my imagination. Honestly, at first it was hard to imagine holding His hand, or leaning my head on Him, or accepting His fatherly kiss on my forehead.

Now, I can easily picture running to Daddy Almighty's embrace. Nothing feels better than to cling to Him and bury my face in His heart; a safe place where I don't have to know all the answers; where I don't have to do it all on my own; where I don't have to smile and act like everything is ok. My place in His lap is where I can just be loved because I'm His beloved child.

The Lord will hear your crying, and
He will comfort you. When He
hears you, He will help you.
Isaiah 30:19b (NCV)

Chapter 2

The Results

I am weak and feel as if I've been broken in pieces.

I groan because of the great pain in my heart.

Psalm 38:8 (NIRV)

It is still easier to say that I was broken, but the truth is that I was never whole. I wasn't taught how to live. I survived but didn't thrive. Neglected and left to myself, I developed my own set of negative coping skills. I developed my own faulty way of dealing with my problems as well as how to deal with other people. I didn't trust anyone, not even God. On my darkest days, I was consumed with anger and bitterly lashed out at those who tried to help me. As a result, many gave up on trying to help rehabilitate me.

But Daddy Almighty never gave up. He spoke softly to my heart and mind. He would firmly say "no" or "stop," but then He would show me what to do instead. His persistent, calm authority and patience finally triumphed over my strong will.

At times, I am still tempted to turn back to old behaviors, but I have now learned to run to Daddy Almighty each time I am tempted to do things my own way.

"For I know the plans I have for you," says the Lord, "plans for well-being and not for trouble, to give you a future and a hope."

Jeremiah 29:11 (NLV)

Trauma led me into losing my desire to live. I had survived, but no longer fought to live. Instead, I fought to die. I was angry and couldn't see past my pain. I didn't see any hope, any future, any chance of finding healing from the trauma of my past.

Finally, after multiple suicide attempts had failed, I realized that God wasn't going to allow me to end my life. All my plans had failed, and I was at the worst point in my life.

It was here, at the end of myself, that I began to surrender to Him and His plans for my life; plans I couldn't see or even imagine. Each day now held a choice to believe that He had the best plans for me. A choice to trust that He knew me better than I knew myself. A choice to follow Him. He sees my future and tells me it's prosperous and worth hoping for.

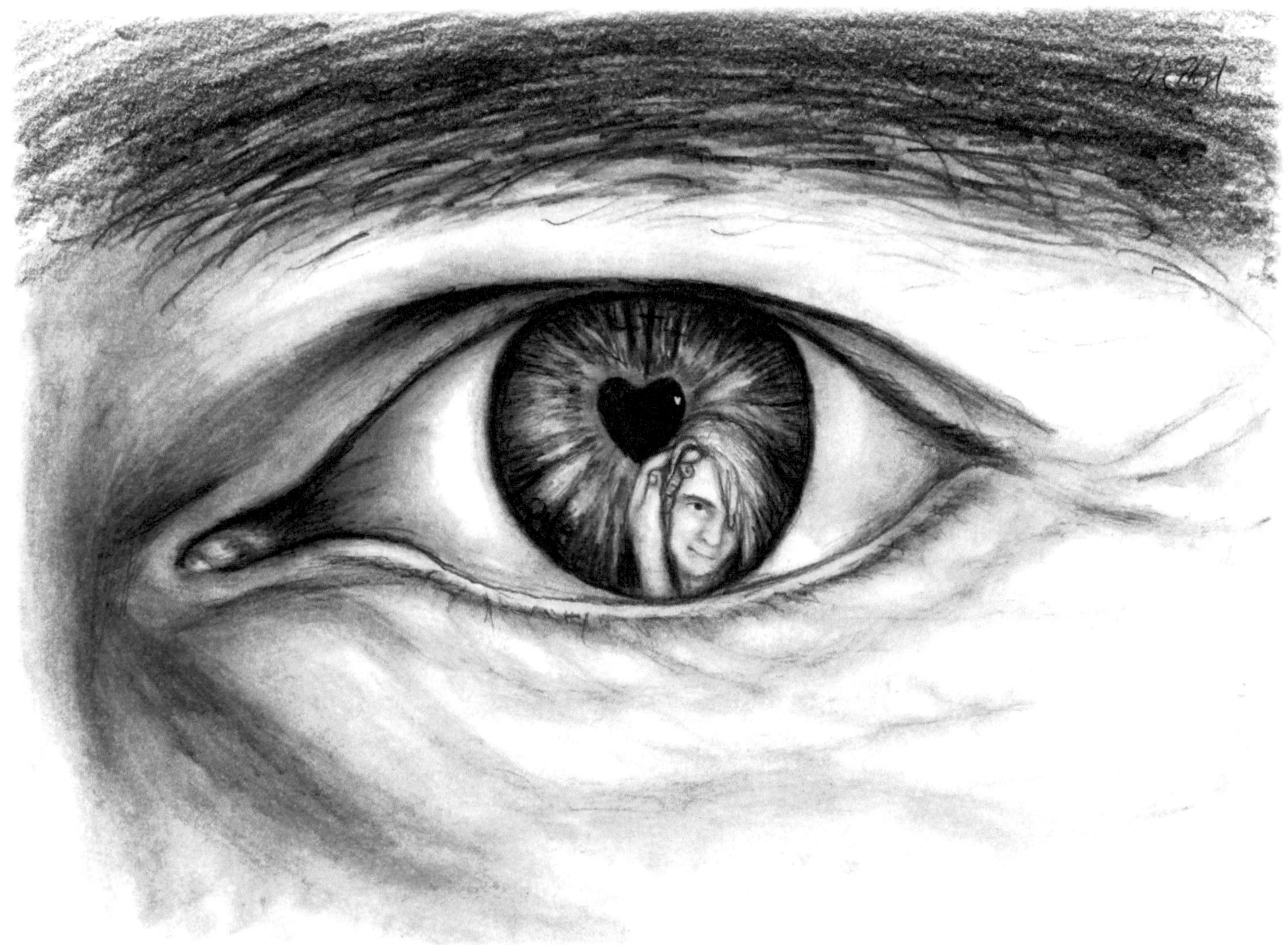

He found them in a desert. It was a windy, empty land. He surrounded them and brought them up. He guarded them as those he loved very much.

Deuteronomy 32:10 (ICB)

You know all my ways very well.

Psalms 139:3b (NLV)

My response to the abuse I suffered was to act out in negative behaviors. I kept people at what I perceived was a safe distance from my heart. Unfortunately, it also prevented those who could help me from reaching me. The lie I believed was that it was better to act "bad" rather than to try pleasing people, only to fail at not meeting their expectations. This tactic worked very well with people on the outside trying to look in . . . but fails

every.single.time

with the One that lives within.

He wants all of me. All of my ways, the good and the bad, the sad and the glad, the loving and the mad. When I "act out," His response is to pull me closer to His heart. He reveals to me again and again that His love is always unconditional, that my behavior has no power to manipulate or change His love for me.

"Lord,

you know everything

there is to know about me.

You perceive

every movement of

my heart and soul,

and you understand

my every thought

before it even

enters my mind."

Psalm 139:2 (TPT)

But he was pierced for our rebellion, crushed for our sins. He was beaten so we could be whole. He was whipped so we could be healed.

Isaiah 53:5 (NLT)

I have struggled with self-harm more than I want to admit. The practice of self-harm began out of two lies that I had believed since my childhood. First, I believed that if I was punished enough I would behave better. Second, if I could hurt on the outside as much as I hurt on the inside, I would feel better. But God revealed to me this truth: it didn't matter how horribly I hurt myself, it was never enough.

Self-harm can easily be hidden from others, but not from Daddy Almighty. It grieves His Spirit deeply when I turn to self-harm instead of Him. And so He gently asks me if He should suffer more for my sins. If He should receive another beating. Or if His flesh should be cut open by a whip one more time. And He gently reminds me that only He, the One who has never sinned, can pay the price for my sin-debt. Absolutely nothing I do will ever be enough.

I have learned that my self-harm is completely unnecessary because my debts__ all of them, past, present, and future, have been paid in full. He paid the full price because He doesn't want me to suffer the punishment I deserve.

Salvation is His greatest gift of love to me. It's an insult to even think that it isn't enough for my sins. Self-harm doesn't just hurt me, it also hurts the One who gave His life for me.

God's grace has saved you because of your faith in Christ. Your salvation doesn't come from anything you do. It is God's gift. It is not based on anything you have done.

Ephesians 2:8-9 (NIRV)

Suddenly, a man with leprosy
approached him and knelt before him.
"Lord," the man said, "if you are willing,
you can heal me and make me clean."
Jesus reached out and touched him.
"I am willing," he said. "Be healed!"
And instantly the leprosy disappeared.
Matthew 8:2-3 (NLT)

Untouchable is how I felt as a young adult. I remember the doctors instructing the residential staff and therapists to not have any physical contact with me because I had been sexually abused by both male and female. I'm sure now that the decision was made for my own protection in my vulnerable state, but at the time, I interpreted it in a negative way.

Silently I observed other clients receive hugs, pats on the back, or a gentle reassuring squeeze to the hand. I felt so alienated, so untouchable. I had always prayed to be loved, to feel love, and now I believed that I would never know what a hug is supposed to feel like. Would I never experience a supportive pat on the back or the closeness of a friend's hand? I thought that I had been ruined for life. I actually believed that the doctors were correct in what they had instructed the staff and therapists. So, for several years I wouldn't accept physical contact from anyone.

Can you then imagine my confusion when after those years of believing the lie that I was untouchable I walked into a church where people I didn't even know wanted to greet me with a hug . . .

. . . like wide opened arms complete embraces with a little squeeze that revealed a heart bursting in joy hugs?

And these children of God were extremely persistent in their pursuit to share His unconditional welcoming love in a tangible way with me.

It took quite a while for me to accept the hugs, but when I finally accepted a warm embrace, I was surprised that I didn't shatter into a thousand pieces. My mind didn't even flood with memories or flashbacks, and I was truly dumbfounded by how much I liked to be hugged. I now count every hug as a tangible embrace from Daddy Almighty. I'm thankful for every one of His vessels who are overflowing with His love, and for His insistence in leading them to be His hands and feet.

By this everyone will know that you are My disciples, if you have love and unselfish concern for one another.
John 13:35 (AMP)

For the Eternal One says, "Instead of a wall of stone, I will be a wall of fire

protecting her all around, and I will be the shining glory within her."

Zechariah 2:5 (VOICE)

I built a wall around me. Each brick I carefully cemented in place. Every single one contained a rule I had set in stone. Many different rules were added in a futile attempt to avoid being hurt. I set in place rules of etiquette in pursuit of social acceptance. Do this, don't do that. Go here, stay away from there. Try these, avoid those. Every mishap, every mistake, meant yet another brick to painstakingly set in place. Life behind my self-built wall became darker and darker until I was barely living at all. I no longer believed that love was true or even real. I eventually came to the place where I no longer felt real. I was a lost soul just moving through the motions, hidden beneath a fake persona, trying to please the world.

When I became too weary of trying to please the world, I started trying to please God. I'd read the Bible with a self-measuring stick and fall dreadfully short of "good enough." I cowered beneath every sacred Word without understanding. I hid in the back pew of the church, sinking lower and lower under the weight of my sins. Believing I was a sinner destined to burn in eternal fire, I doubted He would ever call my name.

But He did.

I was lost, but the Good Shepherd came to rescue me. Daddy Almighty called out to me in my darkness. Brick by brick He tore down my stone-cold wall, demolishing every misconception and lie I believed. The beauty of His grace began to illuminate within me. With loving tenderness, He whispered, "My child you were never created to hide in the dark." Embracing me close to His heart, He proclaimed that in the light of His mercy I am most certainly good enough. He lifted me out of my dark prison and shielded me with His loving compassion. I rejoice because His glorious grace is forever brighter than my shortcomings, so much brighter than every worldly opinion.

This is what the Eternal One says, the One who does the impossible, the One who makes a path through the sea, a smooth road through tumultuous waters.
Isaiah 43:16 (VOICE)

My mind was like a jumbled chaos of images and snippets of memories. As a child I had separated myself mentally from most of the abuse as it occurred. Because of this I struggled with believing and accepting what had been done to me. It was difficult for me to speak about what I saw in my mind. I was afraid that saying it out loud would make it too real to me. I was afraid of remembering more than I already did. Flashbacks were an unwelcome interruption of everyday life, as the chaos in my mind was often louder than my determination to move forward in life. I felt trapped and powerless over everything inside my mind.

This is how Daddy Almighty taught me to give Him everything. He told me to look at everything in my mind as photographs and video clips. He told me to focus on the fact that the images needed to be released from my mind regardless of how they got there. Then as I placed image by image into His hand, He had me envision Him walking into the scene, picking me up, and carrying me out of it. He made a way for me to let it go, to let everything go. I now see Him carrying me through a tidal wave of pictures and memories, as I rest peacefully in the safety of His arms.

You have seen it, for You observe trouble and grief, to repay it with Your hand.
The unfortunate one entrusts it to You; You are the helper of the orphan.

Psalm 10:14 (MEV)

*Do not allow this world to mold you
in its own image.
Instead, be transformed from the inside
out by renewing your mind.
As a result, you will be able to discern
what God wills and whatever God finds
good, pleasing, and complete.*
Romans 12:2 (VOICE)

The world only taught me how to act and how to interact with other people in order to appropriately function in society. But a performance of life is really just that, an act. I felt empty on the inside, hollow, and unreal. I wasn't sure who I was. I thought that I must be unacceptable if all I was doing felt like an act or a pretense. But Daddy Almighty saw His beloved child hiding behind every mask. He didn't come to watch me perform. He came to reveal my true identity in Him. He came to teach me how to live in truth, His truth.

By now I've learned thought patterns don't simply change overnight. Hearing truth for the first time doesn't automatically erase all the lies. Learning what behaviors I shouldn't do doesn't teach me what to do. Choosing to love doesn't instantly heal the wounded heart. The mind has to be retaught by repetitively saying, believing, and walking in truth. It is a slow, continuous process with the occasional pit stop.

It is a moment-by-moment choice to believe I am a child of God, saved by His grace and mercy. I have to keep choosing to believe His Word over my own self-criticism, as well as the opinions of others. I need to remember all "fall short of the glory of God (Romans 3:23 NIV)", and thankfully, He still wants every one of us.

Chapter 3

The Healing

I hear the Lord saying, "I will stay close to you, instructing and guiding you along the pathway for your life. I will advise you along the way and lead you forth with my eyes as your guide. <u>So don't make it difficult; don't be stubborn when I take you where you've not been before. Don't make me tug you and pull you along.</u>

<u>*Just come with me!"*</u>

Psalm 32:8-9 (TPT, emphasis added)

I chuckle every time I read this scripture because I now know that Daddy Almighty's love for me is more than enough to drag me out of a pit and pull me in the right direction. I can be quite stubborn, but His love is supremely more persistent than my stubbornness. I'm not really proud of my defiant ways. I am now being reparented by Daddy Almighty. It has been difficult to unlearn the behaviors I developed in response to the abuse I suffered as a child. His correction is only part of my healing journey. He exposes each lie I believed so that it can be replaced with His truth. He also reveals that His love and presence were always with me in my past and will be with me every day of my life.

For you are my safe refuge,

a fortress where my enemies

cannot reach me.

Psalm 61:3 (NLT)

I didn't grow up in a Christian home. I actually didn't know very much at all about God. However, in every home I lived, every state, every country I moved to, there would be a hiding place of a rooftop, a bush, a tree in a patch of woods, or at times in a corner of my mind. Each hiding place kept me safely away from other people.

The solitude brought tears I needed to release and then a calming peace to my aching heart. The quietness awakened my imagination with comforting pictures and thoughts. The stillness stirred a welcoming sense that I belonged somehow, somewhere, to Someone.

I would leave my hiding place with a restored hope that helped me to keep on living. And although I didn't understand it at the time, I now know it was indeed His Spirit whispering to my heart, mind, and soul. He provided every hiding place. He made sure there was a place of escape from my enemies. He made sure it was isolated enough for me to sense His presence. In every hiding place He would hold me close to His heart as I wept, and He soothed my soul with the thoughts and images of being wanted, accepted, cherished, and loved. He still does this when He takes me to that safe hiding place of His presence. He always has, and will, be my refuge.

The Lord is close to the
brokenhearted
and saves those who are
crushed in spirit.
Psalm 34:18 (NIV)

Then if you cry out to me in time of trouble, I will rescue you, and you will honor me.

Psalms 50:15 (NCB)

. . . I want you to trust me in your times of trouble, so I can rescue you . . .

Psalms 50:15 (TLB)

We live in a world that wants a diagnosis and a treatment plan. It saddens me greatly to remember that for such a long time I allowed diagnoses and labels to define me. When someone asked what I struggled with, I'd rattle off a long list like I was the most pitifully doomed person in the world. To make matters worse, whenever I failed to improve with a recommended treatment, either a new diagnosis would be made or the specialist would just give up. I would lose a little more hope for healing each time. I felt damaged beyond repair. I struggled to believe that I would ever be "well."

In sheer frustration I cried out to God, "What is wrong with me? Why isn't anything helping? What is it that I really have?"
He answered softly, "Me. You have Me, my child."

Read that again. And again. I didn't need a diagnosis. I had God! His power to heal is all that matters. I needed to turn more to the Healer who never gives up on me, no matter how many times I stumbled into the same pit. I needed to rely on His definition of me, His beloved child. And choose to listen to His "treatment plan."

Thus, I began a habit of being still with my Lord every night. I would read, write, listen to Christian music, or draw to connect with Him. This led to writing what I believed He was showing me or saying to me. I would then make sure whatever I received lined up with Scripture.

When I stopped looking to the world for answers and turned in faith to God, true inner healing began.

Reassure me; let me hear you say, "I'll save you."

Psalms 35:3b (MSG)

*That he might sanctify
and cleanse her with the
washing of water by the word.*

Ephesians 5:26 (NKJV)

I struggled with feeling tainted, ruined, like damaged goods permanently stained by abuse. These wounds, although invisible to the human eye, caused a deeply rooted sense of shame that sometimes seemed unreachable and untreatable. The filth of them clung to me.

Daddy Almighty then explained that what others have done to me doesn't define me. With complete knowledge of who I am, inside and out, He reminds me that I was made to be honored and cherished. Although it is difficult for me to imagine being treated honorably, I've chosen to believe it as His truth. He reminds me His words of truth expose every lie and cleans every stain.

I will

sprinkle clean

water on you

and make you

clean

from all your idols

and everything else

that has defiled you.

Ezekiel 36:25 (GNT, emphasis added)

My times are in Your hands.
Free me from the hands of those
who hate me, and from those
who try to hurt me.
Psalm 31:15 (NLV)

Every moment of my life is in His hands. That truth is just as comforting as it is bewildering to me. With an attitude of accusation, I have often cried out, "Why didn't you protect me?" Although his answer to that question might well be beyond my total understanding, He did reveal that He was protecting my soul and spirit that will live for all eternity with Him. My body was wounded, my heart broken, and my mind distressed. But my soul and spirit still rejected what happened to me, so that I knew the trauma was wrong, and not something I should do to others. Rejecting the wrongdoings is my proof of His protection.

I have learned that the past can't change, but my perspective of the memory can. When my mind recalls a memory, I can choose to see Daddy Almighty pick me up and carry me out of that time. He is eternal. He is timeless. The enemy will taunt me by saying, "God wasn't really there for you; you didn't see Him then." In truth, I'm no longer in the past. I am restricted by time, God however, transcends time. When I look back now, I can see Him there. I can see that in His Hands He delivered me from the evil done in that time, and in all times.

FRIDAY
2
1980 80
SUN MON TUE
In all their distress he
too was distressed, and
the angel of his presence
saved them. In his love
and mercy he redeemed
them, he lifted them up
and carried them all the
days of old.   Isaiah 63:9

"For I will heal you. I will heal you where you have been hurt," says the Lord, "because they have said that you are not wanted."

Jeremiah 30:17 (NLV)

Scars make me feel marked, branded by abuse. They are a visible reminder of how much I was hated and treated as worthless. The critical voices from long ago echo from the jagged valley of scar tissue. The marks taunt me in condescending tones that question my true identity.

I wrestle between keeping my scars hidden from others or exposing the depth of pain I suffered. I want to forget everything that was done to me, but I also long for the comfort I didn't receive when the wounding happened. The memories remain long after the wounds heal and scar over. The pain of it lingers beneath what the eye can see.

Daddy Almighty wants to bind up every wound. Not even the smallest scratch passes unnoticed by Him. Of course He already knows what happened because He is omnisciencent. When He asks about a scar it is so He can reveal His healing comfort to me. There are times I can talk easily to Him about a scar. Then there are the times that I have no words. Only my tears speak to Him. Tenderly He touches or kisses every scar and the healing begins. Again and again, He tends to the pain hiding beneath my flesh. There is no limit to how many times I need to see His nurturing. He will keep nurturing me until all I remember when I look upon the scar is His tender loving care.

I will search for my lost ones
who strayed away, and I will
bring them safely home again.
I will bandage the injured and
strengthen the weak.
Ezekiel 34:16 (NLT)

But no weapon
used against you will succeed.
Isaiah 54:17a (NIRV)

Doubt sneaks in as a weapon, slowly poisoning my mind.
In the midst of the doubts peace becomes harder to find,
Recalling all the failures, mistakes, and disobedience combined,
The enemy hisses loudly, "You deserve no mercy of any kind."
My soul searches for some understanding, left undefined.
I start to feel like nothing good about me is real; all is fake
I hate how I am, how easily my faith can shake.
Why do I sin, why don't I just obey?
How many more commands will I break?
Now I'm doubting that I hear You, Lord;
what a foolish mistake.
I am so confused by what I think You say,
How can You love me when I keep choosing to disobey?
Why would You forgive me when I keep going astray?
Oh Lord, why aren't You tired of me wanting my own way?
Could You really love me even when I'm like this?
Or is what I hear just more hopeful foolishness?
Please tell me I'm wrong, that my mind has just gone amiss.
ABBA! I need You; will I ever stop this craziness?
"You can stop now my child," I think I hear You say.
But why would You speak to me when I keep turning away?
It's so hard to believe You really love me in any way.

"Beloved," He says, "My love isn't based on
any behavior you display . . .
Even in the dark cloud of doubt, I will answer your heart's cry,
Your sins are paid in full, for all the times you have,
and will, rebelliously defy.
My child, faith is believing even when you don't understand why.
Now fasten on the belt of truth, so your soul can be realigned,
Wear this breastplate of righteousness,
rebuking temptation of every kind.
Walk forward with the gospel of peace, leaving your folly behind.
You do hear me my child . . .
Take up the shield of faith to cover your mind.
Freely accept this helmet of salvation; without doubt,
YOU ARE MINE,
Draw the sword of the Spirit, my Word,
and true peace you will find.
Be brave, my child, it is a battlefield far beyond mere imagination.
Run to me, again and again, choosing to take My hand.
You won't be fighting alone; by your side I'll always stand.
And just when the battle feels like more than you can withstand,
Trust that I'm carrying you,
far beyond what you can understand."

So use every piece of God's armor to resist
the enemy whenever he attacks, and when it
is all over, you will still be standing up.
Ephesians 6:13 (TLB)

My child,

don't reject the Lord's discipline,

and don't be upset when he corrects you.

For the Lord corrects those he loves,

just as a father corrects a child

in whom he delights.

Proverbs 3:11-12 (NLT)

This picture is very comforting to me because it reminds me that His discipline is perfectly loving. He doesn't respond to my childishly stubborn behaviors with angry yelling or infliction of physical pain. Nor does He engage in my arguments of wanting my own way. He doesn't send me away until I can get over myself. No, His response is a quiet and firm instruction to sit at His feet, to be still until I'm willing to let go of what I want and open my ears, mind, and heart to His way. As I sit at His feet wrestling with my will, He gently covers my mind with His hand. A hand that will never leave me. A gesture that reminds me He still wants me by His side, and He still loves me in my brokenness. Sometimes I sit at His feet for long periods of time.

Daddy Almighty has endless patience that by far waits out my stubborn pride. When I finally humble myself and surrender to His ways, His correction is loving. He doesn't just chastise my behavior or disobedience. He also takes the time to talk to me about it. He helps me see what deeper need I'm trying to fulfill or what I'm trying to hide or mask under my actions. I am always forgiven, but when I need to learn a better way, He teaches and leads me in the right direction. I find security in knowing that my behaviors don't exasperate Him or cause Him to give up on me.

Listen to counsel, receive instruction,
and accept correction, that you may
be wise in the time to come.

Proverbs 19:20 (AMP)

He brought them out
of their gloom and
darkness and
broke their
chains.

Psalm 107:14 (NCV)

He will wipe away every tear
from their eyes.
There will be no more death, sadness,
crying, or pain.
All the old ways are gone.
Revelation 21:4 (ICB)

Daddy Almighty is the light that illuminates the darkness to dispel it. His light brings out whatever I've hidden in the dark, not to shame me, but to free me from its grip. He breaks every chain that attempts to confine or define me. He takes every grievance, every flaw, and every sin that I surrender to Him and extends forgiveness to me. He is all I need to hold onto. He holds the key to my heart.

When he was verbally abused,
he did not return with an insult;
when he suffered,
he would not threaten retaliation.
Jesus faithfully entrusted himself into the
hands of God, who judges righteously.

1 Peter 2:23 (TPT)

I do struggle to forgive, especially when a person repeatedly and purposefully offends me. Daddy Almighty commands me to forgive. I confess that I often do not feel like, or want to forgive. But forgiveness is a choice, not a feeling. My feelings can be strong and overwhelming, but they are not always right. My feelings can be fickle and fleeting, whereas truth is constant, everlasting, and never changing. Truth tells me to forgive and not to take matters into my own hands. Truth tells me there isn't any room for unforgiveness in my heart.

I can choose to forgive even when I don't feel like forgiving. In obedience to Him, every time I remember an offense I can choose to say, "I forgive______________." I don't want to be the judge of another, and I am grateful that I don't have to carry the weight of another's sin. I can leave it all in His hands.

"*Beloved,*

don't be obsessed with

taking revenge,

but leave that to God's

righteous justice.

For the Scriptures say:

If you don't take

justice in your own hands,

I will release justice for you,"

says the Lord.

Romans 12:19 (TPT)

When doubt, anxiety, or fear consumes my mind, I turn my focus to Daddy Almighty's truth. I picture Him holding me close to His heart and whispering into my soul. His still small voice soothes and calms me as He whispers truth into the battle raging inside me.

I love you unconditionally

"I will be a true Father to you, and you will be my beloved sons and daughters," says the Lord Yahweh Almighty. 2 Corinthians 6:18 (TPT)

I have loved you with an everlasting love; Therefore, with lovingkindness I have drawn you and continued My faithfulness to you. Jeremiah 31:3 (AMP)

Don't be afraid, I am with you always, and I am for you

The Lord himself goes before you and will be with you; he will never leave you nor forsake you. Do not be afraid; do not be discouraged. Deuteronomy 31:8 (NIV)

You are not lost or forgotten

Fear not, for I have redeemed you; I have called you by your name; You are Mine. Isaiah 43:1 (NKJV)

I am praying for you

God, the searcher of the heart, knows fully our longings, yet he also understands the desires of the Spirit, because the Holy Spirit passionately pleads before God for us, his holy ones, in perfect harmony with God's plan and our destiny. Romans 8:27 (TPT)

I delight in you

I was there, close to the Creator's side as his master artist. Daily he was filled with delight in me as I playfully rejoiced before him. Proverbs 8:30 (TPT)

You are beautiful, wonderfully made

My darling, everything about you is beautiful, and there is nothing at all wrong with you. Song of Solomon 4:7 (NCV)

My beloved spoke and said to me, "Arise, my darling, my beautiful one, come with me." Song of Solomon 2:10 (NIV)

I praise you because you made me in an amazing and wonderful way. What you have done is wonderful. I know this very well. Psalms 139:14 (NCV)

What I tell you now in the darkness, shout abroad when daybreak comes. What I whisper in your ear; shout from the housetops for all to hear!

Matthew 10:27 (NLT)

Chapter 4

The Promising Truth

For the source of your pleasure is not in my performance or the sacrifices

I might offer to you. The fountain of your pleasure

is found in the sacrifice of my shattered heart before you.

You will not despise my tenderness as I humbly bow down at your feet.

Psalm 51:16-17 (TPT)

I cannot look to the world to sufficiently fulfill any of my desires or needs. Even though I am saved by my Lord, I will still have trouble living in this world. The enemy will taunt me. Evil will still happen. I will struggle with temptation and sin. By His grace, I will surrender it all at His feet and accept that these things are beyond my understanding. I walk in faith and choose to cling tightly to Daddy Almighty's promises to restore all that's been lost.

Fear not, for I am with you; be not
dismayed, for I am your God.
I will strengthen you,
Yes, I will help you,
I will uphold you with
My righteous right hand.
Isaiah 41:10 (NKJV)

I struggle with insecurity. I wrestle with fear. I panic in conflicts. I choose to be meek just to avoid confrontations. His Word tells me not to lean on my own understanding, but sometimes I still struggle to believe that Daddy Almighty is fighting for me and protecting me. It really doesn't help when the enemy recites a long list of instances in which I could easily perceive myself as unprotected.

I know that I live in a fallen world and that I will have trouble in this world regardless of how much I try to avoid it. These two pictures illustrate the truth I'm striving to believe. No matter what takes hold of me to drag me down, He won't let go. He is stronger than any force that tries to pull me down and He will come to lift me back up to Him. I belong to Daddy Almighty. I am hidden in Him. I desire to be so confident in His protection that I would dare to taunt the enemy when he attempts to attack me.

The LORD will fight for
you; you need only
to be still.

Exodus 14:14 (NIV)

I will be your

God

through all your lifetime,
yes, even when your
hair is white with age.
I made you and
I will care for you.
I will carry you along
and be your Savior.

Isaiah 46:4 (TLB, emphasis mine)

I remember that as early as when I was five years old, I was told that I was too big to be carried, to sit on someone's lap, to lean on someone's shoulder.

Hearing these things caused me throughout my childhood to struggle with misperceptions of my size and body weight. I believed that I was overweight, even though I was average in size. I believed that I could only receive comfort if I was small enough. I felt hopeless in my struggles because I knew that I was able to lose weight, but I couldn't lose height.

I now relish the truth that I will never be too big or even too old for Daddy Almighty to love and to carry. When I'm tired, sad, or just want comfort, I will always fit into His big strong arms.

And you saw how the Lord your God cared for you all along the way as you traveled through the wilderness, just as a father cares for his child.

Deuteronomy 1:31 (NLT)

Even then
You will be there
to guide me;
Your right hand will embrace me,
for You are always there.

Psalms 139:10 (VOICE)

I've shared my struggles to remember that God is with me in the midst of trouble, and this is especially true when it concerns my daughter. In the pain of heartbreak over her suffering, I often feel alone, distant and silent.

I forget to pray as fear and worry creep into my soul.

I forget to put on the full armor of God. I become weary in my own rapidly failing strength.

I'm so grateful that when I need Daddy Almighty the most, He doesn't just stand by waiting for me to get my act together and turn to Him. No, He's already there before the first tear slides down my face. He told me that my heart cries out to Him long before I'm able to utter the first word in prayer. He hears my heart long before I can remember that He's holding both my daughter and me in His hands and close to His Heart. How comforting to know that His help isn't contingent on my actions, or the lack of them.

My flesh and my heart may fail,
But God is the strength of
my heart and my portion forever.
Psalm 73:26 (NASB)

The Lord is my shepherd, I lack nothing. He makes me lie down in green pastures, he leads me beside quiet waters, he refreshes my soul. He guides me along the right paths for his name's sake.

Even though I walk through the darkest valley, I will fear no evil, for you are with me; your rod and your staff, they comfort me. You prepare a table before me in the presence of my enemies.

You anoint my head with oil; my cup overflows. Surely your goodness and love will follow me all the days of my life, and I will dwell in the house of the Lord forever. Psalm 23 (NIV)

You

hide them in the

shelter

of your

presence,

Safe from those

who conspire

against them.

You

shelter

them in your

presence,

far from accusing tongues.

Psalm 31:20 (NLT, emphasis mine)

They do not belong to this world

any more than I do.

Make them holy by your truth;

teach them your word,

which is truth.

John 17:16-17 (NLT)

There are many things that are beyond my understanding. I don't see clearly or know a lot of things for certain. I still don't have answers to some of my lifelong questions. But I have learned that it is when I doubt that I struggle the most. And so, I've had to let go of knowing things for certain, and of my desire for tangible proof. I've accepted that God will remain mysterious. Nevertheless, I can still dream, hope, picture His love for me, and choose to hold onto faith without sight until I am home in His house, where I truly belong.

In the same way, we can see
and understand only a little
about God now,
as if we were peering at his reflection
in a poor mirror;
but someday we are going to see him in his
completeness, face-to-face.
Now all that I know is hazy and blurred,
but then I will see everything clearly,
just as clearly as
God sees into my heart right now.
There are three things that remain—
faith, hope, and love—
and the greatest of these is love.

1 Corinthians 13:12-13 (TLB)

But I trust in your unfailing love;
my heart rejoices in your salvation.
Psalm 13:5 (NIV)

Even when chaos surrounds me from every side, I can take refuge in Him who dwells within me. I don't have to understand or know exactly what is happening around me, or worry about the outcome, because I know the Lord is bringing His perfect will to pass. I don't have to make an appointment or go to a meeting place to be with Him. I don't have to wait until He has time for me. He's there even before I speak His Name. I don't have to worry about calling on Him too often. He won't accuse me of being too needy. I don't have to justify my need to ask for His help. Daddy Almighty is always willing to help, always willing to comfort, always ready to pour out His unfailing love.

. . . *the Lord's unfailing love surrounds the one who trusts in him.* Psalm 32:10b (NIV)

Like a toddler, you'll be held, carried, nourished, and comforted.
Isaiah 66:12 (VOICE)

I learned that there is usually an unmet desire behind most misbehavior. To curb meltdowns and fits when my daughter was a toddler, I taught her to tell me when she wanted more attention. She would come to me, reaching her arms up and say, "Me 'tention,' Mommy." I would stop whatever I was doing and give her the attention she craved. Some people might think this would spoil a child, but it didn't. It gave her permission to just want my attention. She learned that she didn't have to act out or have a specific reason to want my attention.

Her desires for attention made me realize that my own belief about asking for attention was often measured by my need more than desire. I thought I had to be hurting, sick, or have something that was wrong. I believed I couldn't receive attention or comfort unless it was in response to a true need. It didn't occur to me that it would be okay to just want a little extra attention, just like my own little one needed from me at times.

I'm certainly not immune to an occasional meltdown amidst life's demands. There are times I feel like an overtired, disgruntled toddler that just wants to feel secure again. Daddy Almighty taught me to come to Him for the attention I seek. All I have to do is turn my thoughts and my attention to Him to see Him waiting with arms open wide. Wrapped securely in a blanket of love with my mind resting on His heart, His unconditional love has the power to make me peacefully calm.

Perfect, absolute peace surrounds those
whose imaginations are consumed
with you; they confidently trust in you.
Isaiah 26:3 (TPT)

The steps of the God-pursuing ones
follow firmly in the
footsteps of the Lord,
and God delights in every step
they take to follow him.

Psalm 37:23 (TPT)

So many paths, so many steps taken, and so many more steps to take. All those steps reflect the craziness I feel but when I focus on Daddy Almighty, I have nothing to fear. He knows the right path for me. He will lead me. I don't always like the next step. I don't see the next step clearly most of the time. I have to trust Him beyond my own understanding. I must choose to believe that what looks like craziness to me, makes perfect sense to Him. It is on that ledge of uncertainty that my faith can either grow or falter.

Daddy Almighty waits patiently for me to take a leap in faith. I envision the leap is like jumping out of a swing without any fear. I trust that He will catch me or scoop me up off the ground to brush the dirt off my knee and kiss it, making it all better.

Either scenario ends with me in His loving hands.

You see,
every child
of God overcomes
the world,
for our faith is the
victorious power
that triumphs
over the world.

1 John 5:4 (TPT)

Chapter 5

The Truth of My Identity

Thus we have been set free to experience our rightful heritage.

You can tell for sure that you are now fully adopted as his own children because God

sent the Spirit of his Son into our lives crying out, "Papa! Father!"

Doesn't that privilege of intimate conversation with God make it plain

that you are not a slave, but a child? And if you are a child,

you're also an heir, with complete access to the inheritance.

Galatians 4:6 (MSG)

I have struggled to recognize my identity. I have often felt "less than," unwanted, and unloved. My perception of self was developed in an environment of traumatic dysfunction. In my journey with Jesus, I have come to know that my identity isn't what I do, where I have been, or what others have done to me. It can be found in what my Lord and Savior has done for me. My Lord draws me close and whispers that I am His. I am chosen. I am enough. I am wanted. I am Daddy Almighty's girl.

Mirror, mirror on the wall, you say I'm not the fairest one of all.

You throw judgement at my reflection. Nothing seems fair in your rejection.

Mirror, mirror on the wall, can you really see me at all?

You say I'm not first or even second best. You say I'm worthless and no one of interest.

Mirror, mirror on the wall, you criticize my every slip, my every fall.

Your ridicule is so shallow, so petty. You toss around accusations like confetti.

Mirror, mirror on the wall, you call me an outcast, an oddball.

All you really see is my appearance. You make assumptions from a single glance.

Mirror, mirror on the wall, I despise the endless errors you recall.

You've kept a record of each mistake. You care nothing about the hearts you break.

Mirror, mirror on the wall, you are the biggest hypocrite of all.

Spewing lies full of deception, from nothing more than a reflection.

Mirror, mirror on the wall, your definition of me means nothing at all.

I'm reminded that beauty is only skin deep. From your discriminating lies I will no longer weep.

Mirror, mirror on the wall, it is my name I hear my Savior call.

My Lord says I'm precious and honored in His sight! And for my soul He promises to always fight.

Mirror, mirror on the wall, God says you will be demolished in your fall.

His vengeance is coming for all you've done wrong, and compared to eternity your wait isn't long.

So goodbye forever, mirror, mirror on the wall.

I'm leaving you in your dark and desolate hall. I walk now in Christ's forgiveness and mercy.

And His beloved child is the only reflection I see!

*The Lord
does not
look at the
things people
look at.
People look
at the
outward
appearance,
but the Lord
looks at
the heart.*

1 Samuel 16:7b (NIV)

Still, Eternal One,
You are our Father. We are just clay, and
You are the potter.
We are the product of Your creative
action, shaped and formed into
something of worth.
Isaiah 64:8 (VOICE)

I used to pretend to be someone else every time I moved to a new house, a new place, or a new school. In each relocation, I would eagerly replace who I had previously been with what I believed was a new opportunity to better portray a person who could gain approval and acceptance.

The world's critical opinions of me had become my internal dialogue. Even though I now know that the opinions of others aren't truth, this dialogue returns every time I know that I have done something wrong. Daddy Almighty, however, wields a hefty sword that swiftly divides truth from lies. When I forget who I really am, tidal waves of scriptures flood through my mind to wash out every single lie.

These Scriptures remind me:

Even though I fail . . . I'm not a failure,

I make mistakes . . . but I'm not a mistake

Romans 3:23 . . . All have sinned and continually fall short of the glory of God,
but through faith I have been justified freely by His grace

Isaiah 43:4 . . . I am precious and honored in His sight

1 Samuel 25:29 . . . I'm His treasure that He keeps in His treasure pouch

Jeremiah 31:3 . . . I am loved with an everlasting love and drawn
with loving kindness

1 John 3:1 . . . I am His beloved child

It doesn't matter what the world says. It doesn't even matter what I say. His Word is greater! His truth is all that matters. He says that I am valued. I matter. I am one of a kind. I'm not meant to be someone else. I am His masterpiece intricately designed to only be ME.

For we are God's masterpiece.
He has created us anew in Christ Jesus,
so we can do the good things
he planned for us long ago.

Ephesians 2:10 (NLT)

The Lord is like a father to his children,
tender and compassionate . . .

Psalm 103:13a (NLT)

Why would I draw an image of Jesus bathing a nude child? I'm asked this question often, so I will explain what it means to me. As a child I never felt okay being nude. Nudity meant being hurt or defiled, or spoken of in ways that brought shame. It felt like my body wasn't mine but belonged to everyone else to do with as they wanted.

Daddy Almighty has told me that I should not have been treated in this way, and He gave me this image of bathing a child. He explained that a loving caregiver honors a child's body and doesn't focus on the child's nudity. A bath is given with the purpose of cleansing the body. A bath also signifies being taken care of.

I have never felt like the child in the image, but I am intrigued by it. I study her calm demeanor and I study Jesus's face as He gazes upon her. And I feel no fear as I realize this is how He saw me as a child . . . a precious little girl deserving to be cherished, honored, taken care of, and loved unconditionally.

The gaze of a truly loving parent will always pale immensely in comparison to the Lord's unfailing love. When He looks at His child it is always with eyes full of love. His focus isn't on our nakedness or shame or failures. His focus is on our hearts, where He sees His cherished creation's reflection on His own heart.

He is love __ pure, unconditional love.

As a mother

comforts her child,

so will I

comfort you . . .

Isaiah 66:13a (NIV)

Love the Lord your God with all your heart and with all your soul and with all your mind.

Matthew 22: 37 (NIV)

When I spend time in Daddy Almighty's presence, sometimes He tells me to portray Him with a kiss. It seems like just a small act of affection and is often very difficult for me to do when I'm agitated or angry. But it proves to be powerful in helping me to adjust my attitude, because it brings to my remembrance how loving He is. Everything He does is done in love.

When I remember the price, He willingly paid, I become more willing to let go of any of the grievances I had intended to complain about. I often think that there isn't really anything of great value that I can give to my Savior in return for His great gift of grace to me. He asks me to give Him myself, my heart and my love. It is love that He values and desires.

Because of Christ and our faith in him, we can now come boldly and confidently into God's presence.

Ephesians 3:12 (NLT)

I delight greatly in the Lord; my soul rejoices in my God. For he has clothed me with garments of salvation and arrayed me in a robe of his righteousness.

Isaiah 61:10a (NIV)

The Lord your God is with you.

The Mighty One will save you.

The Lord will be happy with you.

You will rest in his love.

He will sing and

be joyful about you.

Zephaniah 3:17 (ICB)

He pursues me tirelessly. He finds me even in the deepest of pits. I often ask why. I do not see what He sees in me, but He says that He wants me. It is hard for me to fathom that someone just wants to be with me, not to be sought for what I can do. It is difficult to comprehend that someone wants to hear my thoughts and listen to what's in my heart. Although I lack experience in receiving such unconditional love, Daddy Almighty tells me His love is always within my reach. This truth makes me long for Him, for His comfort, His acceptance, and His everlasting love.

I was in awe the first time I watched an artist paint Jesus live onstage while the church sang praises to our glorious Savior. My friend asked if I could do that.

My response was, "Oh no, I could never do anything like that."

A few years later the director of the music ministry at my church, Pastor Dave, asked me to paint live onstage with the choir and orchestra for the Palm Sunday services. He strongly believed I could do it and encouraged me to try. I prayed about it and asked the Lord for three confirmations to affirm that I should try. I got seven confirmations within that same day, but Daddy Almighty suggested that I should draw rather than paint Him.

Before that first performance I practiced again and again, never feeling quite confident, but still choosing to trust Daddy Almighty.

I stood nervously in front of my drawing board that first time onstage. On the cue of the first note, I picked up my chalk, and the world slowly faded away. Daddy Almighty took my shaky hand and led the way. I sang my praises to Him as my chalk danced across the board. All that mattered in those moments was the illustration of His great love, the same gracious love He continues to reveal to me.

You will be a blessing to others. Do not be afraid.

Let your hands be strong so that you can do my work.

Zechariah 8:13b (NIRV)

Chapter 6

The Answered Prayers and Blessings

But I pray to you, Lord. So when the time is right, answer me and
help me with your wonderful love.

Psalm 69:13 (CEV)

Though I've had a lot of trials and tribulations, I seek to turn my focus on the many blessings and prayers the Lord has answered in my life. Every day I pray for the needs of others as well as my own, and then leave those requests in His hands. I count my blessings and thank Daddy Almighty for everything good I can think of. I don't ever want to lose sight of His goodness in the midst of living day to day in a fallen world.

Whatever is good and perfect comes to us from God.
He is the One Who made all light.
He does not change. No shadow is made by His turning.

James 1:17 (NLV)

They will not labor in vain, nor will they bear children doomed to misfortune; for they will be a people blessed by the Lord, they and their descendants with them.

Isaiah 65:23

I remember the day I was told that I wouldn't be able to have children. I was twenty-seven years old. I remember going swimming later that same week at a nearby lake. My desire that day was to either wash away the bad news or drown in my sorrow. Suddenly, screams of fear interrupted my pity party. There was a large family at the lake that day and one of the older children had put a toddler in the water on a floating chair. The chair had carried the baby out to the middle of the lake and no one in the family knew how to swim. As I swam out to try to rescue the baby, I was praying that the toddler would stay on the chair and not disappear into the murky water. Every time I got close to the baby, however, the chair would float a little further away. Near exhaustion, a thought came to my mind urging me to swim under the water to the other side of the chair in order to create waves that would move the chair toward the beach. The terrified mother waited with open arms as the chair finally bobbed close enough for her to grasp her baby. She thanked me and I went my way.

I didn't think much about that day until four years later when I was camping at the same lake, just shy of seven months pregnant. My back hurt from sleeping on a cot, or so I thought. After swimming in the lake, my water broke, and my precious daughter was born ten weeks premature in an ambulance. She wasn't breathing on her own at first, and she struggled with feeding, jaundice, and apnea. She was three days old before I was allowed to hold her. I felt as though I was holding my breath the entire six and a half weeks she was in NICU. I didn't feel worthy of such a wonderful gift, a gift far better than any I had ever received before. Like the mother who was terrified for her baby four years earlier, I was so afraid of losing mine. I was overwhelmed with more love for my miracle baby than I had ever felt for anyone or anything before.

But you have received the Holy Spirit from God. He continues to live in you.
So you don't need anyone to teach you. God's Spirit teaches you about everything.
What he says is true. He doesn't lie.
Remain joined to Christ, just as you have been taught by the Spirit

1 John 2:27 (NIRV)

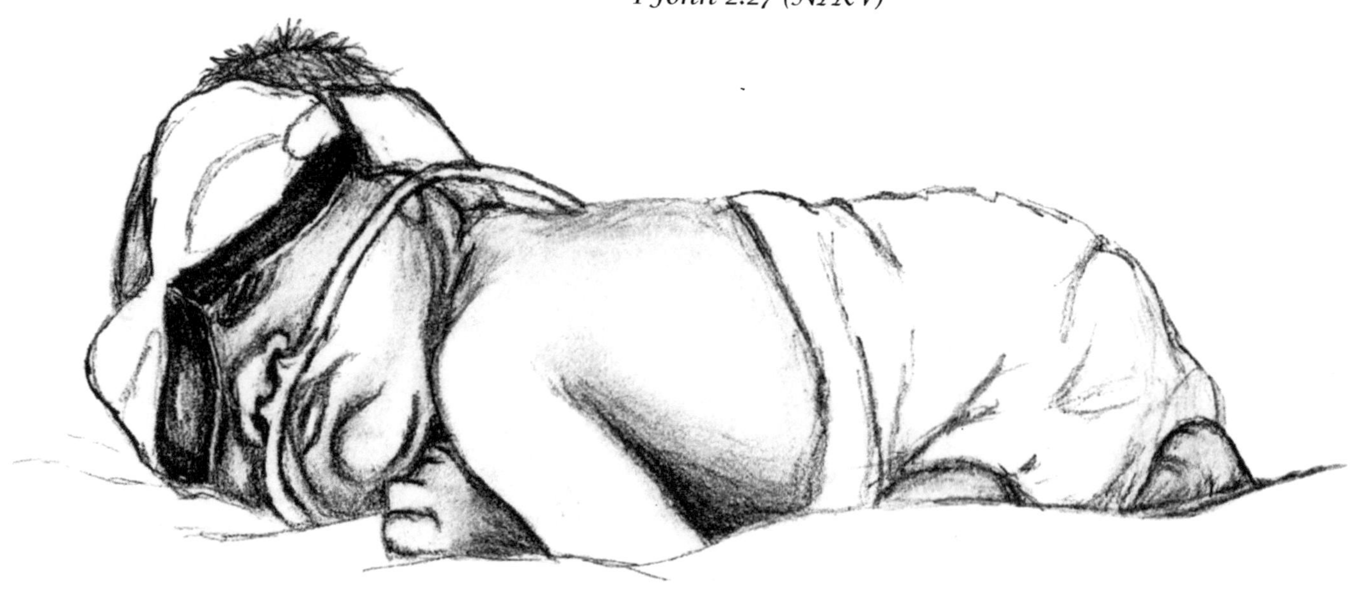

My daughter's birth came as a tremendous blessing accompanied by a time of great tribulation. Her father and I separated shortly after her birth. She required a lot of extra care, and several of our family members didn't believe I could be a competent parent. I wasn't so sure either. All I knew was I didn't want to fail. I lived in fear, a crippling fear that I might lose the precious gift of my daughter. A deeply rooted anger and resentment from all the hurt I had experienced accompanied that fear.

For two years I put on a steel armor, hammered and sealed with anger and mistrust, I plastered on a fake smile. I acted like everything was fine through every doctor appointment, physical therapy, speech therapy, occupational therapy, and appointments with vision impairment support services. I was exhausted. I felt like I couldn't ask for help or even admit that I needed it from anyone.

Thankfully, in spite of all of this stubborn independence, Daddy Almighty gave me grace to hear from Him. I would cry out to Him and admit that I was terrified of failing to be a competent mother. I really didn't know how to be a good mother, but I prayed for His help. As always, He answered. He comforted me and taught me what I needed to know. He would remind me of the comfort I craved as a child and used those memories to help me to look closely at my daughter and see what she craved. He awakened my motherly instincts. The Lord assured me I was the best mother for my daughter.

In many ways my daughter and I grew up together. She recently turned seventeen as I write this, and it is bittersweet. I'm going to miss her when she leaves for college, but I'm so amazed and grateful for her strength, courage, and faith in the Lord. I know I'm biased, but she truly is a living, breathing miracle of God.

He will once again fill your mouth
with laughter and your lips with shouts of joy.
Job 8:21 (NLT)

Jesus said, "For judgment I have come into this world,
so that the blind will see and those who see will become blind."
John 9:39 (NIV)

My daughter, Kaytlyn, was born with a rare genetic eye disorder called Aniridia, which is the absence of the iris __the color part of the eye. Her vision continues to deteriorate a little more each year. I know she will have perfect vision someday, either in this world or in heaven. I also know that she is fearfully and wonderfully made, intricately handcrafted by our Heavenly Father. It may or may not be His will for her vision to be restored in her time spent in our fallen world.

I share all of that because many people choose to respond to impairments with pity or despair, and sometimes even ridicule or scorn. But I choose to see the blessing that my daughter is as God created her.

Daddy Almighty taught me to focus on Kaytlyn as a whole and not focus on sight alone. I learned to let her try just about everything she believed she was capable of doing. I'd comfort her when she failed and joyously celebrated every victory with her. She is stubbornly independent and then some. I'm thankful for her perseverance. Because Daddy Almighty taught me not to place limits on her she has accomplished much already. She dances in our church dance ministry, serves on the youth tech team, swims like a fish, and strives to be a standup comedian. She has even been an international award-winning artist several times since she was five years old.

Kaytlyn truly is so much more than her visual impairment!

For we walk by faith, not by sight.
2 Corinthians 5:7 (NKJV)

They were terribly insulted and horribly mistreated;
now they will be greatly blessed and joyful forever.
Isaiah 61:7 (CEV)

It is incredibly difficult to hold onto hope and faith when losses and tribulations seem to outweigh blessings. My first marriage failed before my daughter's first birthday. The people closest to me doubted that I was mentally capable of raising my daughter alone. I felt vulnerable to the world again, often feeling abandoned by Daddy Almighty even more than I had as a child. I felt cheated because I had followed His Word. My first husband and I had courted and refrained from intimacy before marriage. We attended church regularly. I believed we'd be together until death. He had promised to help me raise our daughter. He failed. I failed. But I was in the process of growing in the knowledge that Daddy Almighty never fails!

As I longed for a partner to share life with, I remember people advising me to search online dating sites. My reply was always the same: no thank you, I'm not looking. My prayers, however, were different. I prayed for the godly man Daddy Almighty wanted for me. I didn't want to choose a man. I wanted Him to choose one for me. I believed that if it was the Lord's will, He would bring the right one into my life.

I waited almost fifteen long years. It wasn't easy. It was often lonely and depressing. But Daddy Almighty knew when I would be ready to really love again.

Daddy Almighty chose a godly man from my church. I had first met him at a Palm Sunday service where he sang in the choir while I drew a picture live onstage. Later that same year, I saw him at a Celebrate Recovery meeting. I discovered he was broken as well, recovering from divorce and depression. Neither of us was ready at that time to pursue a relationship. It was eight years before we finally met for coffee. I had always prayed to be loved for who I am and not just for what I can do. I didn't realize that prayer would be answered with two long years of courtship. My future husband was determined to form a relationship completely void of physical contact until marriage __completely. It was eighteen months before he even held my hand. I was elated when he finally proposed!

My husband believes in chivalry and has taught my daughter and I to wait for him to open the car door for us. He reminds us that we are precious and should be treated honorably. He calls me darling and nicknamed our daughter DJ which stands for "darling junior."
We just celebrated sixteen months of marriage in May, 2023. We are happy and enjoy having our Helper by our sides.

God decided in advance to adopt us into his own family by bringing us to himself through Jesus Christ. This is what he wanted to do, and it gave him great pleasure.

Ephesians 1:5 (NLT)

I was seven years old the first time I ran away from home. It was a week before Christmas, and I felt so hated and unloved that I decided to go look for a new family. In the middle of the night, I slipped quietly out the front door. I had left a note on my pillow telling my family that I was going to an orphanage because they didn't love me, and I was leaving to find a new family. As I stomped through the snow, I fought back tears. In my mind's eye, my young imagination began seeing "little monsters" in the snow, and I began to carefully watch my steps in order to avoid walking on them. As I struggled to avoid the monsters my soul heard a soft whisper telling me, "Go back home." I finally turned and ran back home that night. Years later, Daddy Almighty revealed to me there were much bigger monsters in life than the ones I had been running away from that night.

Looking back, I realize I was disappointed that God wasn't answering my prayers the way I wanted Him to or when I wanted Him to. Because I wasn't trusting Him to provide a loving family, I was trying to find one on my own. For many years, I searched for a new family. Even as an adult I kept looking for a place to belong. I moved approximately every two years, believing the next place I lived would finally provide relationships that gave me a sense of belonging.

I moved to Pennsylvania when my daughter was four years old. Two years later, I was ready to move again. But the school district opened a vision support classroom with five other visually impaired students. This meant my daughter would not only be mainstreamed, but she would also have educational supports and fellow classmates who also experienced vision problems.

I stayed for my daughter, but Daddy Almighty began opening doors for me as well. He led us to a church family, a Celebrate Recovery family, an amazing group of family friends, and to my new husband. For the first time in my life, I lived in the same house for over twelve years! My daughter and I laughed because when we moved into our house, I said we wouldn't be there long since we were on the second floor. Along with that we had no yard, no off-street parking, and no washer or dryer hookups!

I now know that Daddy Almighty made me a part of His family before I even knew Him in an intimate, personal way. I'm so grateful that I belong to His family. In His perfect timing, He has abundantly answered my prayer. I thank Him every day for all of the families I'm a part of now!

But the Lord says,
"Do not cling to events of the past
or dwell on what happened long ago.
Watch for the new thing I am going to do.
It is happening already— you can see it now!
I will make a road through the wilderness
and give you streams of water there."
Isaiah 43:18-19 (GNT)

I had a traumatic childhood. I had many viable reasons to terminate family relationships. But I didn't. With Daddy Almighty leading the way, I followed Him closely to walk in forgiveness. It wasn't easy, and it often didn't seem fair. I stopped complaining about how I had been treated. I stopped rehashing it. I stopped expecting apologies. I stopped seeing my family members as I had perceived them in the past, for Daddy Almighty began showing me who they are now!

First, I will share about my earthly father. Being in the military he was gone most of my childhood and we moved often. As an army brat, I lived in countries where disabled children like my own daughter were abandoned and left to die. If these children did survive, they were destined to be beggars on the streets. For many years, I resented the military for hindering a close relationship with my dad, but now I'm grateful for how God has used all of my experiences and insights into other cultures to mold me into who I am today. And I'm grateful for not only my father's service, but for all of the soldiers who have served and fought for our freedom.

It is a tremendous blessing to see my father now as a grandfather, or as Kaytlyn affectionately calls him, her Papaw. She is Papaw's girl. They have a special bond. He is her hero, and she is his angel.

One special memory I treasure is when Kaytlyn was first released from the hospital. She had to be fed every three hours and held upright for an hour after each feeding. It was exhausting! And what a blessing when my dad would get up an extra hour early before leaving for work at five o'clock in the morning and hold her upright for me so I could get a little more sleep.

When she was seven years old, Kaytlyn created a collage, "Dancing With Papaw," that won first place in the InSights Art competition through the American Printing House for the Blind. She told me I couldn't tell anyone until she told Papaw. Later that evening, she called him and excitedly whispered in the phone, "We won first place, Papaw."

I enjoy seeing how loving my dad is with her. I like to believe that when I was a little girl, if he had not been so overworked, stressed and tired, he would have been better able to show how much love he had for me. I look at him with Kaytlyn and feel blessed to witness and now comprehend his love language.

Now all things are of God, who reconciled us to Himself through Jesus Christ, and has given us the ministry of reconciliation.

2 Corinthians 5:18 (NKJV)

. . . bless and show kindness to those who curse you, pray for those who mistreat you.

Luke 6:28 (AMP)

I didn't believe that my mother loved me. I grew up convinced that she hated me. I thought that I was always underfoot, in her way. I was too loud, too whiny, or too big. I didn't feel pretty enough. My dirty blonde hair tangled just by looking at it. I had big "buggy" eyes with dark circles under them and a nose that dripped constantly from allergies.

"When you finally learn that a person's behavior has more to do with their own internal struggle than it ever did with you . . . you learn grace." __ Allison Aars

I thank Daddy Almighty that He has spent a lot of time through the years revealing to me the ways that my mother communicates her love. Now, when I look back at my mother in the past, I can see that she loved me in her own way.

My mother is very creative, and this is highlighted in her thoughtful gift giving. I remember as a child my favorite gift was a Victorian-style dollhouse kit she had my dad put together for me. She created furnishings for every room, completely matching and color coordinating them. I spent many hours playing with that dollhouse, imagining a world inside of it that I would love to live in.

I also cherish an extensive set of fine chinaware she bought for me. During my teenage years, I remember her visiting the military post gift shop every week for four years to collect more of the imported matching pieces.

My mom is also an excellent seamstress and good at crafts. Throughout my childhood she made me dresses, dolls, and even created beautiful items to decorate my room. Today, she enjoys sending Kaytlyn and me what she calls "I love you" packages with homemade cookies or a movie with candy and popcorn to enjoy as we watch it.

I can't change other people, but I can yield to the changes the Lord wants to make in me. He has helped me change how I see my mom. How fitting it is that she chose butterflies as the pattern for my chinaware because they represent transformation. Daddy Almighty has certainly transformed me, opening my eyes to see my new identity in Him, and to see others also through His eyes.

Bear with each other and forgive one another
if any of you has a grievance against someone.
Forgive as the Lord forgave you.
Colossians 3:13 (NIV)

The Party

You have been chosen, cordially invited
To the party of your lifetime recited
No, no there's no need to bring anything along
Actually, to be so kind would be well, kind of wrong.

For this party you won't be needing a reservation
For you'll party someplace without much specification
This kind of party tends to take place just about anywhere
So, there's no need for such details, it's a very informal affair.

You'll know it's time to party when negativity sets in
You can party solo or find a couple of friends to drag in
It's really up to you as to when the party starts and ends
But it's definitely crashed when any positive crap begins.

Don't worry you'll know how to party at a party like this
Remember just do and say everything with a negative emphasis
Bring up and rehash all the past that seemed so wrong
Then dance around to that old familiar tune of your sad, sad song.

Most importantly, this party will be all about you
Bygone days and days you have yet to live through
You will be the center of all the attention, no really
You can accept this invitation at any time to your....

Pity Party

Being cheerful keeps you healthy.
It is slow death to be gloomy all the time.
Proverbs 17:22 (GNT)

In my late twenties I wrote this satirical poem to remind myself of "what not to do" when I'm feeling overwhelmed and when my thoughts go spiraling down the memory path of grievances. I allow myself to grieve or focus for a short while on a problem, but I don't allow it to consume my life.

So, what do I do instead? My answer is simple but powerful. First, I pray and give it over to Daddy Almighty. Then I start listing out loud the people God has placed in my life and the things I'm thankful for, no matter how trivial they may seem to be. Lastly, I remind myself of all the prayers He has been faithful to answer. I especially remember all the times He has revealed to me that He was at work during the storms, even when I couldn't see Him.

My brothers and sisters, think of the various tests you encounter as occasions for joy. After all, you know that the testing of your faith produces endurance. Let this endurance complete its work so that you may be fully mature, complete, and lacking in nothing.
James 1:2-4 (CEB)

For God so loved the world
that he gave his
one and only Son,
that whoever believes in him
shall not perish but have eternal life.
For God did not send his Son
into the world
to condemn the world,
but to save the world
through him.

John 3:16-17 (NIV)

Do you remember the little girl in the tree at the beginning of my illustrated journey of healing? She desperately wanted to be someone else, someone who belonged, someone who felt loved and accepted. That girl was me. I didn't see it then, but Daddy Almighty had begun answering prayers from that first time I cried out to him from the top of a tree.

The Lord already had me in His hands. He had already chosen me to be his child. My Heavenly Father knew everything about me before I took my first breath. The harm that would be done to me. Every trial and mountain I'd face. How many times I'd run away from Him. Every time I'd rebel and disobey. And He still wanted me enough to die for me.

I have often wondered, what did He see from the cross? He told me that He saw every single struggle and sin as He hung on that cursed tree and took His last breath. And then He gave me this image of Him looking down from the cross at a child at the foot of the cross, one of his beloved little ones who desperately needed and wanted their Savior.

You will be satisfied with a full life
and with all that I do for you.
For you will enjoy the fullness
of my salvation!

Psalms 91:16 (TPT)

Who could ever separate us from the endless love of God's Anointed One?

Absolutely no one!

For nothing in the universe has the power to

diminish his love toward us.

Troubles, pressures, and problems are unable to

come between us and heaven's love.

What about persecutions, deprivations, dangers, and death threats?

No, for they are all impotent to hinder omnipotent love…

So now I live with the confidence that there is nothing in the

universe with the power to separate us from God's love.

I'm convinced that his love will triumph over death, life's troubles, fallen angels,

or dark rulers in the heavens.

There is nothing in our present or future circumstances that can weaken his love.

There is no power above us or beneath us— no power that could ever be found in the universe that

can distance us from God's passionate love, which is lavished upon us through our

Lord Jesus, the Anointed One!

Romans 8:35, 38-39 (TPT)

About the Author

Mae grew up in a military family that lived in several different countries and in a number of states all across America. She has an associate degree in art and works as a self-employed illustrator, muralist and portrait artist. She utilizes her gifts volunteering in the church by making costumes, dance overlays, paint props and backdrops for the Children's Dance Ministry, Choir and Theater Group, as well as drawing live onstage for the Orchestra, Choir and Praise Team. She resides in Pennsylvania with her new husband and teenaged daughter. In the past ten years Mae has had the privilege to portray through her gifts the love and healing grace that God offers to the world.